Published by Ad Hoc Fiction.
www.AdHocFiction.com

Purchasing Information:
Paperback available from www.AdHocFiction.com
E-book available from all usual outlets.

Printed Worldwide.
First Printing 2021.

ISBN paperback 978-1-912095-35-3
ISBN e-Book 978-1-912095-34-6

THINGS I CAN'T TELL AMMA

by

Sudha Balagopal

For my daughters

Contents

Things I Can't Tell Amma 1

Quail with a Topknot 5

The Missing "I" 9

Help Wanted 13

A Letter from Amma 17

How I Make Colors Fade 21

What's-His-Name 24

The Kiss on My List 28

Pumpkin Pie 30

Roving-Tentacle Hands 34

Theo 37

Mirror Ornament 40

Benjamin Franklin 43

Another Letter from Amma 47

Bridge Across Oceans 50

About the Author 57

Acknowledgments 59

Things I Can't Tell Amma

March 27th, 1981

I twist the curly wire connecting the rotary phone's receiver to its base. My first call to India from 9,000 miles away.

Amma will say, "This call must be costly. Write letters, except when there's news." She'll ask if I'm eating and sleeping. Then, as an inveterate matchmaker, she'll push the "eminently suitable" Mrs. Pai's son in California.

There are things you can tell your mother, and there are things you can't.

I can tell Amma that the traffic in America is orderly and quiet, that I open a bank account and get my phone connection in one day, that I can use an amazing new device—the automated teller machine—to withdraw money instead of going to the bank.

I can't tell her that my flight arrives late, that I take a cab from the airport at 11 p.m., that the apartment office is closed, leaving me no place to go, that Theo, a young American wearing metal-rim glasses and what she would consider inappropriate, faded-denim shorts, offers to let me stay with him, that I sit outside the office

all night, that I watch male students in togas—fake
Greeks in white sheets tied around their shoulders—
cavort to loud music across the street, that I wait
there until morning, when people walk past me as if
a travel-worn Indian woman settled on her suitcases
is an everyday occurrence, until Theo with the metal-
rim glasses hands me a mug of lukewarm black coffee
and asks if I'd like to freshen up, that he says, "I don't
have a gun, I promise," with a sparkly smile.

Or, that I run my tongue over slimy teeth.

March 29th, 1981

My apartment is next to Theo's. With an ear against the
wall, I listen to his television. His dishes clatter over
the sound of canned laughter. I calculate the hours—
breakfast in India, time for hot idlis with chutney or
peanut-laden aval upma.

When I dial home, the phone rings and rings.
Amma'll ask why I haven't called Mrs. Pai's son, then
contradict herself, ask why I'm wasting dollars. It's
always easier to lie. I prepare to say, "His phone must
be out of order."

I organize my information.

I can tell Amma that the grocery stores here are
massive, that I can get everything except Indian spices,
that I crave her cooking, that I can hear the radio

over invisible speakers in the stores, that the phone company's advertisement asks us to "reach out and touch someone," that it seems like such a nice thing to do, that my studio apartment is tiny and spare—a twin bed, desk, chair—that my department is half a mile away, that I've been clocking the walk there so I can get to class on time, that I bought myself a plasticky jacket because it's cold here in March, that I have to train my ears to understand American English, that I'm confused about the spellings here, that tomorrow is the first day of the quarter, first day of class.

I can't tell her that Theo sees me walking to the grocery store, that he offers me a lift in his car—chipped blue paint and noisy—that the woman on his car radio sings, "Call me," that he laughs, sparkling again, and says, "Hop in," that I decline and end up trudging back with heavy grocery bags draped on either arm.

March 30th, 1981

I ring home for the third time in four days. The phone does not connect. While I try again, I decide if she answers I'll preempt Amma and say, "Mrs. Pai's son doesn't answer his phone."

I can then tell Amma about Dr. E in communications class, that his "annihilation" sounds like "an-eye-lation," that I have lunch at the student union which is big and loud, that they have loads of unfamiliar foods—potato salad, macaroni and cheese, bagels and cream cheese—that there are many television sets, that giggly girls at my table watch a show called *General Hospital*, that a blanket of silence drops when the television screen changes to breaking news, when newscasters announce someone shot the president of the country. And that, I can announce, is the big, shocking news.

I can't tell her that Theo is in the student union, that he slides in next to me, that he drinks cola and squeezes a yellow condiment into his many-layered sandwich, that he catches me staring at his frayed backpack—ready to snap with the weight of its contents—that he grins and starts to unzip his backpack, and at that moment, they tell us a gunman shot President Reagan, that Theo reaches for my hand, that I gulp and gulp, that the giggly girls are silent for two minutes before they start talking about *General Hospital* again.

Nor can I tell Amma that the phone company's jingle repeats in my mind, and repeats and repeats, that there's an echoey silence at the other end of the line, that I understand the Indian telephone company must have disconnected her line because of an unpaid bill, that I must accept she is more miles away than I can count, that I want to tell her everything.

Quail with a Topknot

"There's a bird in the library," I tell the librarian. The university employee has thin, penciled brows and a nest of brown hair.

I place the encyclopedia on her desk. With an unsteady hand I show her the wet splatter of bird dropping—an irregular stain on the information about polling methods. "I need this material for class."

"Maybe where you're from, birds come into libraries. Not in Arizona." Her red-tipped finger indicates the closed windows of the air-conditioned building.

I want to tell her in Calcutta I paid a membership fee to read books about America, that the owner of the corner library kept his windows open, that a myna family lived in the nook above the front door, that he fed them tiny pieces of mango and guava, that they didn't come in. He also fined me if I damaged a book.

She moves the offending encyclopedia away from herself with one finger, studies my embroidered orange kurta, the color of the robes worn by the Hare Krishnas singing in unrecognizable Hindi on the lawn outside. At home, when they roamed Park Street, Amma told me to keep a safe distance.

I spot Theo in the library. He doesn't walk up to the counter to say hello, or tell the librarian I'm a friend.

"What am I supposed to do?" I ask.

"Have you looked through the card catalog? Microfiche reader?"

I ask her for help with the machine. She says she cannot leave her desk.

"It's a little quail with a topknot." I imagine telling Theo about this creature which defiles the book, then hops into my backpack like he's home.

I share an apartment wall with Theo, against which I lay my ear each evening so I can listen to Dan Rather on television. Sometimes, I hear Theo laugh when he watches *Three's Company*. Sometimes, I hear him on the phone, low and intimate. Sometimes, I hear him pop a cassette into his player. Sometimes, "Endless Love" and "Celebration" seep into my apartment.

This is the man who calls himself an eternal student —he's going for his fourth degree—the man who offered me coffee, a ride to the store.

A bit of excrement lands on my shirt because I cannot look away as Theo kisses a girl in the aisle between library stacks, because I'm drawn to his muscled arms on either side of her as she rests against books, because I'm staring at the girl with big hair, tan legs, short-shorts and cork-heeled shoes. Because I'm wondering how it feels to be kissed like that.

"This bird made a mess on my research for the paper on polling methods," I tell Dr. E during office hours. The professor wears a blue-and-maroon checked jacket. The crease of his khaki pants is as sharp as an envelope slitter.

His pink tongue darts out, moistening his lips. When he palms my lower back, I freeze. He refused to accept my last assignment because it was handwritten, even though I'm a foreign student who doesn't own a typewriter. I received a zero—my first quarter at the university off to a bad start.

"That's a better excuse than my dog ate the homework," he says.

My Amma says only goats eat paper.

As I leave Dr. E's office, the department secretary hands me a message slip. "You had a call from a . . . Mrs. Pai's son? Number's here."

"Do you live by a henhouse?" Mrs. Pai's son says on the phone.

The quail squawks louder on my lap.

"He's my bird," I say, stressing the possessive.

Mrs. Pai's son is the man Amma's set me up with. She can't understand why I won't accept her highly suitable choices—three so far—can't understand why marriage and a degree won't happen simultaneously.

I don't ask how Mrs. Pai's son tracked me down. Maybe I should admire his initiative. Maybe Amma knows best. Maybe he'll kiss me like Theo kissed that girl between the stacks.

"Noisy bird!" Mrs. Pai's son says. "Can you get him to shut up?"

I put the animal on the floor, cover him with my laundry basket.

Mrs. Pai's son says he'd like to see my photograph.

I tell him I'm behind on my paper.

He doesn't offer to mail me his picture. Instead, he talks at length about his job at a chip-making company in California, "Not the kind you eat, heh, heh."

I drop bits of apple through the holes in my upside-down laundry basket. Inside the makeshift cage, my bird beats his wings, screaks.

Maybe Theo has an ear against his wall, maybe he's listening to the bird's shrill sounds, this conversation. Maybe he'll pop over, ask to hold him.

"I'm going to India on vacation," Mrs. Pai's son says. "My mother wants a Walkman. I told her I don't have time to go shopping."

The bird's frantic. Mrs. Pai's son is still talking when I hang up.

I lift the laundry basket, cradle my quail, caress his restless wings.

The Missing "I"

"You're late." Gladys, the typist, examines my scrawny handwriting. She licks an ink-stained index finger, flips through the pages. "It'll be twenty-four dollars for twelve pages. Six dollars extra for the rush job."

Theo, my neighbor, referred Gladys. He didn't say she was expensive.

Gladys wears thick glasses; eyes hidden behind their unkind density. A desk crowds the tight room. I'm wedged into a chair, satchel on my lap. Stacks of papers overwhelm her table.

She takes a sip from a large mug. "Please wait while I look this over," she says. "I may need clarifications." Her voice is raspy, as if she has laryngitis. The stench of stale coffee hovers.

I want to tell her many things: I cannot afford thirty dollars; my fingers hurt from writing all day; the professor expects a typed paper; I'll have to drop the class if I receive another zero; international students must maintain the requisite credits; I don't want to return to Calcutta, a failure.

Instead, while she reads, I stare at the typewriters that sit on sturdy shelves.

The gray Remington reminds me of unpleasant typing lessons with the corpulent Mr. Dutta back home. The cloying odor of his hair oil filled my nostrils as he leaned his considerable torso over my table. Every fifteen minutes he came by to remind me, "A, s, d, f, g h." Or, he said. "Qwerty, remember, qwerty."

I didn't complete the course. My college application declares a falsified typing speed of thirty words per minute.

The machines on Gladys' shelves are arranged alphabetically, the green Olivetti between a sleek Corona and a sturdy Remington.

I wonder if Theo owns any of these brands. His machine makes comforting clickety-clacks interrupted by the rough *phrrs* of the carriage return. When I place my ear against the wall separating his apartment from mine, I learn things about him—when he eats, when he wakes, when he's on the phone.

A scrap of paper taped on the Olivetti reads: "For sale."

Gladys encircles phrases, flings the sheets toward me. "What are these words? Write them out in capital letters."

I have six more papers due this quarter.

"How much for that typewriter?" I like green things: green grass, green parakeets, green mangoes.

Gladys drops her pen, clicks her tongue. It sounds like annoyance. "Fifty dollars if I type this paper for you, if not, sixty."

I write her a check for sixty dollars.

The taillights of the bus disappear into the hush of dusk as I arrive at the bus stop.

I sit on the edge of the sun-heated, graffiti-stained bench for thirty minutes. Soon, a dust-laden wind rises, whistles through my hair—an impending Arizona monsoon storm.

I walk the two miles home. Gladys didn't give me a case for the machine. A spritz of rain dampens my hair. Some drops land on the typewriter keys.

It's 8:30 p.m. when I walk into my building. A party's in full swing in the recreation room; strains of "Funkytown" battle the din—never mind it's a Tuesday night. The banner on the wall outside the room reads, "Congratulations, Prince Charles and Lady Diana Spencer: 7-29-1981."

No one else seems to have a paper due.

My quail shrieks as I enter the apartment. I pick him up, caress his wings.

When he quiets, I put him back into his makeshift cage.

Theo's television is silent. Maybe we'll hit our staccato keys in synchrony tonight. He and I held hands once, when we heard President Reagan was shot.

I place an ear against the wall, hear muffled voices, one male, one female. Occasional words waft. "Warm today . . . would you . . ."

I'm certain she's willowy with carefully tousled hair, a hint of moist color on velvet lips.

All night, I type. All night—between the metallic clacks and kerchunks—my ear's trained for noises from next door.

All night, my bird is still, confused by the activity, the bright lights.

I re-read the paper with gritty eyes. Dr. E, my professor, will give me a zero.

As soon as it's daylight, I call Gladys. The phone rings and rings. I imagine she needs her glasses to answer.

"It's early," she rasps. "What d'you need?"

"The typewriter's 'I' is broken, I mean, the letter 'I' doesn't show up on paper."

She clicks her tongue. It sounds like annoyance.

"Just write the damned 'I' in."

She hangs up.

Theo didn't tell me she could be rude.

On the other side of the wall, his television's tuned to *Good Morning America*.

I pick up my pen.

Help Wanted

I eat cold, leftover noodles for breakfast, get to the Student Union at 7 a.m.

The petite girl with the curly black hair snaps purple-colored chewing gum as she fills the newspaper dispenser.

"Hey, magenta, I'm almost done," she says, brown eyes alight.

She's called me turquoise before, the color of my skirt.

I ignore her, grab a copy of *The Campus Sun*, open the classifieds page. Yesterday, I contacted an office about a job posting at 8:15 a.m. They said the position was filled.

I arrive breathless at the basement office—three miles away in a brick building at the farthest end of campus—at 8 a.m. A wizened old man sits at the desk, feeding paper into a noisy machine. Mountains of material—some bundled in twine, some overflowing from boxes—surround him.

"I'm here about . . ."

He cups a hand around his ear.

"I'm here about the job. You need a shredder?" I shout.

He stands tall, all five feet, five inches of him. White hair forms a ring around his bald spot.

"I need a strong young man, someone who can carry fifty pounds." His voice is loud.

"Please, I can shred paper," I yell.

"You're short and you weigh, what, 110 pounds? And that outfit won't do . . ."

"I need this job, please. I can feed paper into a machine."

The old man cups a hand around his ear.

When I call the cafe about the advertised position in the classifieds, the manager schedules an immediate interview.

I find him in the hive of a kitchen, a red-stained apron around his ample middle. He leads me into a room that ought be called a closet.

"Show me your hands." He smells like my dinner from last night—noodles tossed with half a raw onion.

I shove clenched fists inside my skirt's pockets.

"Show. . . me. . . your hands," he enunciates, spacing out the words as if I'm short on comprehension.

I stretch out my arms, palms facing up. "I can do anything, really," I say.

"Sorry." He pokes the flesh under my thumb with a finger. His long nail creates an indentation on my skin.

"Too soft, not used to hard work. I need someone who can handle huge, greasy dishes."

I'm walking across campus when the petite newspaper girl with the curly black hair calls out, "Hey there, magenta!"

Passers-by swivel, their gazes on my skirt. I quicken the pace, slip into my classroom. We're not scheduled to start for another twenty minutes.

Dr. E is at his desk, studying a computer printout, reams of inter-connected paper overflowing from his desk, onto the floor. He waves me in. I slink into my usual seat at the back, open the newspaper, circle advertised positions, wondering if I'm too late to apply for these.

"Looking for a job, huh?" Dr. E stands close. I can smell his dank, woodsy, cologne. The scent irritates my nostrils.

"I need an assistant for a project," he says. "Week-days 6 to 9 p.m., interested?"

I should want to jump. I should want to shout, "I'll take it. I'll take it."

Instead, I remember his hand on my lower back. I push away the internal warning, remind myself, this is a job.

"What's the project?" I ask.

Students stream in.

He leans, a palm on my shoulder; the tone is secret-low.

"Market research. I pay more than minimum wage, five dollars an hour."

I stand. His palm falls off my shoulder.

Amma's letter is in my mailbox. She says she's had her phone reinstated.

I'll call in the evening, tell her I've been improvising with food, flavoring noodles with garam masala. No need to tell her noodles are cheap.

A Letter from Amma

Calcutta
August 20, 1981

Dearest Deepa,

Last night I dreamt my room was on fire. I woke up at 3 a.m. believing giant flames surrounded my bed. My old heart thumped as if I had run up the three flights of stairs to our flat.

Don't worry. I had no pain in my chest or I'd have phoned the doctor.

Anyway, I switched the lights on and peeked under the bed. After that, I sat on the sofa until the milkman rang the bell.

There are at least two hundred books in the built-in-storage under the bed. You didn't know, did you? Nor did your father.

I've told you my parents decided I should get married when I turned eighteen. I was in my first year at college. Your father owned a Chevrolet then, a huge, tan car with brown fins I called wings. You never saw that car. There were few cars in our small town in 1957. My parents thought that your father's family was well-to-do because he owned a car. To me, the ship-sized car was an embarrassment. It blocked all traffic—bullock cart, cycle-rickshaw and pedestrian—in and out of our narrow lane. When he stepped out of the vehicle, the neighbors bowed to my bridegroom-to-be as if he were a prince.

After the wedding, my parents sent me off to Calcutta with many, many gifts. I suppose, today, you'd disdainfully call such presents my dowry: gold jewelry, silver dishes, a radio, the marriage bed, a steel almirah, satin sheets, silk saris and all my books. I've explained to you that those days, parents considered such things a daughter's security. Who knows, maybe the possessions made her worthy of the in-laws' respect.

During the first weeks of marriage, in a wave of tenderness he lost soon after, your father promised I could complete my education.

I never did—not formally.

To my horror, I learned your father had business debts. He paid them off by selling assets—the land he inherited, then the car. Soon, he sold my jewelry. Finally, only my books remained.

One day, he locked me in the kitchen, piled my books on the verandah. I watched as he lit a match and threw the burning stick on the stack, saying, "If these can't be exchanged for cash, they're worthless." I swept the hillock of debris into a copper drum. That container is in the attic.

Oddly, your father offered prayers to Saraswati—the goddess of learning—every Friday. You have seen him do the puja.

How do I have so many books under my bed?

I purchased each one with chippings from house-keeping costs, five rupees here, ten rupees there. Some are used books I bought from the corner library. I studied the stalwarts like Dickens, Hardy, Twain, in stolen snatches of time between scrubbing stains on shirts and ironing wrinkled collars, between dicing potatoes and peeling carrots.

Did you know I was enrolled for an English degree when I had to discontinue?

I'm so proud you're a student in the United States, with the privilege to read anything, really, anything at all. No one can steal this wealth from you.

Last week, after so many decades, I took your grandfather's old Olivetti out of the steel trunk. It sits on the dining table now. I hope you understand why I kept the typewriter shrouded in saris, locked inside. Your father would have sold it. Or worse, flung it from the verandah.

In the past few days, I have been pecking at the keys on the typewriter.

By the way, Mrs. Pai said her son would like to visit you during Christmas. I told her that would be a good idea. You'll like her, she's soft-spoken and kind. I believe a mother's influence shapes what a man will become. You're lucky to meet him. I didn't have any say in who I married. Your father was presented to me and that was that.

Write back. I know I have said it before, don't waste money on international calls.

I hope you are eating and sleeping well. I can see you shaking your head, saying, "You're always concerned with food and sleep."

Of course, I am. I worry about you. That's my job.

Your loving, Amma

How I Make Colors Fade

I'm walking to work, when the petite, curly-haired, bubble-gum-chewing, newspaper girl manifests herself next to me. "Hey, violet."

I tell her not to call me violet. "My name is Deepa. The word means light," I say.

"But I love your skirt," she says.

I can't understand her logic. "I'm not a color," I say.

"Violet is the result of mixing red and blue and now I can see your skirt has those colors too," she says. "Are you an international student?"

I nod. She blows a bubble with her wad of gum.

"You're like a moving garden," she laughs. "A good contrast to the denim and pastels here."

I walk and she keeps pace, tells me she's an intern at *The Campus Sun*. "Can I interview you for an article on your life here?"

"What?" I stop, shake my head. "No. Sorry!"

She says, "Readers will love pictures of you in native costume. All the bright shades . . . "

I visualize my likeness printed on thousands of copies of the newspaper, imagine being recognized everywhere on campus, shudder.

"I don't like being photographed." I pick up speed. If I wasn't wearing slip-on sandals, I'd run.

Somewhat out of breath, she says, "By the way, I'm Carla Payne. Look, I'll get a byline, you get to be in the paper, a colorful win-win for both of us."

"I do not want to be interviewed."

She presses a piece of paper into my palm. It has her number on it.

A week later, when she calls out the color of my shirt—orange this time—in the grocery store, I instruct her to keep her voice down, remind her, again, that my name is Deepa.

"Orange, here in the store, is a fruit. Orange, the color, comes from mixing red and yellow. I am neither," I say.

I'd read somewhere that the color can be a call to action.

At home, I pull all my outfits out of the closet, study the rainbow of garments.

I take a bus to the secondhand clothing store and ask the manager, whose thin mouth is a mere slit on her face, if she'd be amenable to an exchange—my clothes for theirs. She doesn't smile until I show her my turquoise shirt, crimson skirt and a golden-yellow scarf.

I pick achromatic apparel—two pairs of non-descript jeans, a couple of T-shirts, one gray, one olive.

On the way back, I examine the khakis and grays in the quiet bus.

The next morning on my way to the Student Union, I see Carla, The Payne. She snaps her chewing gum as she fills the newspaper dispenser.

I call out, "Hi, Payne!"

She stops, squints, comes closer.

Her eyes go saucer-sized. The color of my jeans matches hers. Exactly.

"Want to get some coffee when you're done?" I ask.

What's-His-Name

"Hi, 211! You have a problem with your stove?" Alan, the super, addresses tenants by their apartment numbers. "Sorry I couldn't come sooner. Had classes all week."

He steps in, boombox atop a shoulder. The two-in-one radio-cassette player has fifteen shiny buttons and is larger than his toolkit.

"What's that?" He tilts his head toward my upside-down laundry basket.

"What's what?" I lift my shoulders.

"Your basket is squawking."

His wide-legged stance is at odds with the cheerful Hawaiian shirt he's wearing.

"No pets allowed. It's in the lease," the twenty-something says with the authority of his position.

My defiant quail screeches.

I lift the basket, gather the creature.

"See? He's small and no trouble. My neighbor hasn't complained about noises."

Alan rests his hands on his hips. "Look, you get rid of what's-his-name and I won't say a word."

I smooth the bird's feathers with my fingers.

Alan waits.

Cradling the quail in one hand, I grab my backpack. Behind me, I hear Alan sing with the jingle on his radio.

Outside, I insert the bird into my partially-zippered bag.

Alan called my bird "what's-his-name."

I vacillate between Moti and Chotu and have pondered American names like Bobby—what's-his-name bobs his head a lot—and a generic Sam. Mostly, I call him Dear. That's how my maternal grandmother addressed my grandfather. She never uttered his name in the fifty years of their marriage. I believed it was the prevailing custom until she told me, "When someone is a part of your soul, you don't need to call them by name."

I hunt for a nook to hide the bird. The machines in the laundry room churn and tumble, the rec room is locked, and the janitor is in his closet.

Theo's car is in his usual spot in the parking lot, distinctive with its chipped blue paint and the partially-open window that doesn't roll all the way up.

Surely, he wouldn't mind.

I squeeze my arm in through the gap, unlock the car.

When the bag lands on the back seat, the surprised bird screaks.

"Good job, 211! You got rid of the bird," Alan says when he sees me. He doesn't mention the missing backpack. "Try these knobs."

I wave a hand over the warming electric coils on the stove. "Thanks."

He steps closer. "Sorry about the bird. How about you and I go see *Raiders of the Lost Ark*?"

He places a hand on my arm. I stare at his black knuckle hairs.

"You're going to like us, TWA," Alan sings as he lifts the player, places it on his shoulder.

I clatter down the stairs. Theo's car hasn't budged. I pause to catch two breaths, peek through the window.

The backpack has moved.

A pair of sunglasses hangs from the visor, an empty soda bottle leans in the cup holder.

No bird anywhere.

I look under the seats, in the pockets of the door, in the glove box.

No bird.

I sink on the cracked pavement by the car, watch a line of ants carry remnants of a dead fly.

The sun sets. It's Saturday night. At the frat house across the street, they're ready for a toga party.

Theo's television is silent. Tonight, I can't abide the thought of make-believe laughter for company while I fail at homework.

I doze, wake at midnight, turn the lights on. No quail.

This morning, the weatherman on Theo's television predicts a cooling trend.

Alan wants to see *Raiders of the Lost Ark*. I'm not sure I do.

I'm making coffee—one spoon instant coffee, two spoons sugar, half a cup of milk—when I hear a scratchy scraping from the window-box outside.

A quail sits in the now-empty container in which my predecessor must have planted flowers.

My soul tells me he's Dear-Moti-Chotu-Bobby-Sam. I cut up an apple, drop in the bits. The quail takes a piece of fruit, flies to the top of a mesquite tree and on to the rooftop of the building opposite.

Other birds join him.

Dear-Moti-Chotu-Bobby-Sam blends into the flock.

The Kiss on My List

I wear the emerald-green kurta to the not-so-surprise party Alan throws for my birthday because Amma mailed the shirt all the way from India, because she spent her hard-saved money on a phone call just to hear my voice, because I miss her treats of rossogollas and cutlets, because memories cause a whoosh of homesickness to swoop through my belly.

I'm saturated with emotion—sodden like the condensed-milk-laden *tres leches* cake on the table— because I'm half a world away from home, because I'm drowning in the frothy affection of people I've known a scant five months, because I feel untethered like the neon-colored balloons bumping up against the ceiling, because I imbibe alcohol for the first time, wine and cheap champagne.

My eyes burn and threaten to spill because the gifts of cookies, flowers and books overwhelm, because I listen to someone sing about a queen of hearts, because I convince myself I can dance, because I tipsy-twirl until my insides spin, because Alan places a sparkly tiara on my head, because my neighbor, has a casual arm across a girl's shoulders, because I envy that closeness.

Of course, a kiss is on my list—along with a visit to the Grand Canyon, whale watching, inner-tubing, and graduating early—because at twenty-two it's something I yearn to experience, because a tender, lips-touching, breath-exchanging kiss would make for a swoon-inducing, head-swirling moment.

So I believed.

Until Alan holds me vise-tight, because he won't let go, because he ruptures my lower lip, because he rips my emerald-green top, because he leaves the fabric in tatters, because I must push hard, because I must shout, "I said, NO."

Pumpkin Pie

8:30 a.m.

I eat pumpkin pie for breakfast. Sara, the department secretary, brought me a generous wedge yesterday. "It's not Thanksgiving without this dessert," she said.

The pie is sharp-sweet with a whiff of cinnamon, a hint of nutmeg and the tang of ginger—quite the opposite of Amma's pumpkin curry with onion, garlic and tomatoes, or her pepper-infused pumpkin dal.

I'm chasing the dessert with sips of coffee—one spoon instant coffee, two spoons sugar, half a cup of milk—when the phone rings. This morning there are no ambient sounds, not even Theo's television from next door, to dampen the harsh ring.

"Shanta here," the lady on the phone says. "I'm your mother's friend."

The voice on the other end crackles with static.

"Yes?" I sift through reasons for this call from India.

When she opens the next sentence with, "Don't worry, but . . ." the pie churns in my stomach.

"I was visiting your mother this afternoon when she had chest pains. I took her to Belleview Hospital."

"Hello?" she says when I don't respond.

"I'll come," I say. "It'll take a couple of days. Tell her I'm coming."

"She thought you might call home and wonder where she is. I'll give you the hospital's number. Ring her tomorrow."

I thank the lady, check my five-dollar wristwatch. It's 9:30 p.m. in India. Eight long hours before I can talk to Amma.

Mid-morning

I fling the remnants of the pie into the trash can, pour my coffee down the drain.

There's no reason to obey my mother's friend.

After several redirects, I reach a kind-hearted night nurse at the hospital who tells me Amma's stable and asleep. The international call lasts half an hour. I refuse to think about the cost.

Amma taught me families are about love.

I open my fridge, stare at the void. The only item that remains is a near-empty quart of milk.

I daren't go to the store in case I miss a call.

3:00 p.m.

I look out through the kitchen window. Theo's car is missing from his spot in the vacant parking lot. Like everyone else, he's probably spending Thanksgiving at home surrounded by the buzz of conversation, the lilt of music, the clank of dishes—the sounds of a family gathering.

The outside window box contains shriveled bits of apple I've put in hoping for my pet quail's return.

I glance at my watch. Too early to call Amma.

5:30 p.m.

The calls fail the first two times I call the hospital. The third time, the operator leaves me in a chill of silence for ten minutes before she connects me.

"Hello?" Amma says.

I relax my tight hold on the receiver. Her voice conveys—tentative, but even.

"Oh, Amma . . ."

"Nurse tells me you called at night. Why are you wasting money on international calls?"

Her chiding makes me smile. "I was worried."

"That was just a scare. Shanta, Mrs. Pai, will take me home this morning. Don't worry."

"I'm coming," I say.

"Nonsense! You stay where you are and study for your finals next week. Focus on the projects you must complete."

"But you're alone, Amma."

She pauses, says, "So are you."

Later, I replay the conversation in my mind, absorb the friend's name—Mrs. Pai.

9:30 p.m.

When I call again, a nurse informs me Amma's been released.

My wobbly knees remind me I haven't eaten since the morning.

Next door, I hear Theo's television, lending the first semblance of normalcy to my day.

Someone knocks on the door.

"Brought you leftovers." Theo's smile sparkles.

I rub the back of my hand against my mouth—swallow.

"Hey, what's wrong?" He places the box on the table, opens his arms.

I rest my cheek against the warmth of his shirt, inhale his scent. He holds and holds.

Roving-Tentacle Hands

I wind the spaghetti tighter and tighter until it clings in a blob to my fork. My gaze is on the man in the crowded cafeteria line.

"Hello!" the Payne reaches across the table, pats my arm. "Hello!"

She follows my stare to the man in the blue-and-maroon checked jacket. His arm snakes across his female companion's back, fingers sliding down to squeeze her glute.

"Who's that?" the Payne frowns. "The man. And who's she?"

I look at my plate, shrug.

"Come on . . ." Payne shakes her head. Her curls bounce on her shoulders.

I study my ball of spaghetti. It won't fit in my mouth.

"I don't know the girl." I drop my fork. "Please, let it go. I don't want trouble."

"Oh my God, does he do that to you?" She digs into her bag, peels a wad of gum, and sticks it into her mouth.

"No. Definitely not. But to others, yes."

She narrows her eyes, snaps the gum in her mouth, blows a bubble.

"Okay, that's Dr. E," I say.

I don't add that I conceal every centimeter of skin when I dress for work, that when Dr. E approaches, I step behind a desk, or that he's forced to keep a distance, because I do.

"Have you told anyone, a higher-up, someone in a position of authority? Why didn't you tell me?"

She's loud.

"Shh. . ." I say. "Look I'm here to study. I can't . . ."

I won't discuss Dr. E's proclivities.

The Payne, when perturbed, chews with gusto.

"I've learned such situations are best managed on my own," I say.

I've never spoken of Alan's aggression on my birthday or my relief on learning the apartment management dismissed him for being negligent with his duties.

My own Amma doesn't know about Mr. Sen. He's the man who lives across the landing from her, the man with the roving-tentacle hands, because of whom I stopped riding the elevator in our building back home.

"Well, if you won't do something, I will." The Payne is saucer-eyed. "I'll write an article about harrassment policies, I'll take it to the higher-ups."

"Please, Payne, please, I cannot get involved."

"You won't." She picks up her tray, leaves.

I sit at the table for another hour. The spaghetti dries and cakes on my plate.

Theo

Sozzled with each other, you and I venture out for coffee at first light, end up eating a meal, nostrils seduced by the fragrance of syrups—old-fashioned maple, boysenberry, strawberry—tongues titillated by the scent of pancakes, hash browns, and lavish swirls of melting butter.

The omelets we order are bursting with the zing of onions, the tart-sweet of tomatoes, and the earthiness of mushrooms.

"May I have some sliced jalapenos?" You request the waitress for the hot peppers I call chilis.

I ask if you're sure and you scoff, "I can handle habaneros. These are mild."

The peppers make you hiccup, your green eyes tear. You take off your glasses, I wipe off the wetness with a napkin.

I ask you to hush when I practice my driving in your car, the dusty blue vehicle with lines criss-crossing the vinyl seats. You turn up the radio's volume, sing louder, something about just the two of us. Your words make my hands tingle, and I pull over, fearful of losing focus. You laugh and turn up the volume, again, then press your fingers into the furrows between my eyebrows to smooth them out. The warmth from your hand meanders like molasses through my body.

"You must learn to deal with distractions." You insist I drive.

"Give me your hand," I say, and bury a kiss into your palm.

We catch a Saturday morning show of *Chariots of Fire* because as you tell me, "Ticket prices are lower if we go before noon."

While I get the tickets you pick up a tub of popcorn, something we don't need since we ate a big breakfast.

"It's tradition," you say.

We settle into the last row. The tub leans on your knees, my handbag hangs from the arm of my seat, and my shoulder rests against yours.

I tell you it's my first time in a movie theater in this country.

And you ask, "Come home with me for Christmas, meet my parents?"

Just like that. No indication, no preamble.

I put my fingers into your tub, feel the fluffy, bumpy texture of the snack.

"I can't. I'm so sorry," I say. "Mrs. Pai's son is visiting me on Christmas Day."

"You really want to meet that guy?" A shower of popcorn spills over my legs, and into the aisle.

"I promised Amma," I say. "I must do this for her."

Your shoulders stiffen and you draw into your seat.

"Are you going to marry him?" you ask.

"No. Of course not," I say.

The movie begins. You press fistfuls of popcorn into your mouth.

I spend the length of the movie, 124 minutes, wishing your arm would pull me close, wishing I could dip my fingers into your tub of popcorn, wishing you'd lick the saltiness off my fingers.

My feet tapping on the floor, I zip and unzip my handbag.

You finish the popcorn, set the container on the seat next to you.

I hug my arms against my chest, seethe against Amma: for trying to arrange my marriage, for not understanding that refusal doesn't mean I don't love or respect her, for letting me go and not letting go of me.

For making it inevitable that I must perplex and distress her.

And, you.

Mirror Ornament

Mrs. Pai's son tells me his mother wants him to marry an Indian girl.

"Girls from our culture are adjustable. Not like Western girls," he says.

A limp, puppet-like doll hangs from the rearview mirror in his car. The ornament's legs and arms are entwined in the string. I reach forward to disentangle the limbs, change my mind, sit back.

Under the odor of his aftershave lurks a new-car smell.

A blue beach towel's draped on the passenger seat; the nubby fabric itches through my shirt.

"Take the man I bought this car from," he says. "Just last month he got this 1982 model for his wife, thinking she'd be pleased. Now she's filed for divorce, says she hates the car and wants the cash instead. Bah, these Western girls."

He strikes the doll on the mirror. She swings agitatedly.

"I've named her Sunny, heh, heh, heh . . . the car, I mean."

The vehicle's a puke yellow.

I wonder if the husband also bought the ornament that droops from the mirror, if the woman looks like the doll—thin arms, thin legs, blobby nose, sad little red-button mouth—whether she felt tied up.

Mrs. Pai's son has a receding hairline and a bulging forehead. He's wearing a sweater in colors that burn my retina: sheeny purple and neon green.

I tell him nothing's open on Christmas day except a cafe that serves twenty-four-hour breakfast. I rub my throat to ease the squeeze of betrayal—it's our place, mine and Theo's.

He parks Sunny far from other vehicles as if she's too superior to hobnob with regular cars.

Before he gets out of the automobile, he straightens the beach towels on the seats. Outside, he uses his handkerchief to wipe the car's hood, touches his lips to the car's nose.

Mrs. Pai's son says, "Gentle with the door, Sunny doesn't like to be slammed."

He orders a hard-boiled egg, one slice of toast and a decaf to which he adds three sugars. When he slices into the egg, the gooey yellow streams onto his plate. He commands the waitress to get him a replacement.

"*Yeh ladkiyan ullu hoti hai,*" he says. These girls are stupid.

While waiting for his egg, he lathers his toast with butter and grape jelly, tells me he gets the best deals.

"Like the car?" I ask as I pay for the meal from my meager college-student earnings.

He drives me back to my apartment.

"Do you like my vehicle?" he asks, striking the doll hanging from the rearview mirror.

I want to tell him the towel itches my back.

"Yes, it's nice," I say.

He places a rough hand on my upper arm, pulls, then smites a moist kiss on my ear.

I rub the back of my hand against my ear before reaching for the doll.

I yank her off the mirror's stem. Cradling her against my chest, I step out of the car.

Benjamin Franklin

Sara, the department secretary, calls and says, "Dean Wise wants to see you at noon."

A foreboding skitters its way up my spine. I should never have said anything to my friend Carla—The Payne—about Dr. E's inappropriate behavior. She's pursuing an exposé.

Although she promised not to mention my name, I've received a summons.

Dr. E is my professor, thesis guide, and employer. He pays me after work every other Thursday. Last night he gave me two notes in a plain white envelope, a hundred and a twenty. I examined the hundred-dollar bill ten times—a single piece of paper worth nine thousand six hundred rupees in Indian currency, eight months of rent for Amma's flat. In Calcutta, if I rode the tram, or went to New Market with this much money, a pick pocket's nose would smell the notes and his slithery fingers would swipe the cash in seconds.

I choose my clothes with care: jeans, white full-sleeved shirt, closed-toed shoes.

Sara, the secretary, doesn't look up from stapling papers. "Dean Wise is expecting you," she says.

I clutch my backpack, palms sweat-moist, fingers ice-chip cold. My final project is due in two months.

Dean Wise leans back in a poofy chair that squeaks under his body's weight.

"Sit," he says.

Curtains of gray-black hair on either side of his balding forehead remind me of the picture of Benjamin Franklin on the hundred-dollar bill. His jowls vibrate as he speaks.

"You worked for Dr. E?" His voice is gravel rough as if abraded by years of smoking. The ceramic ashtray on the desk holds a sprinkling of debris.

I hug my knees and ankles together.

"Yes. I still do." When I bite my lip, I cut into an old rupture, taste blood.

In my time here, Dean Wise—academic royalty— has bestowed upon me no more than an occasional nod.

I flex my toes inside my pumps. My shirt is a sheath of heat.

There are two other females working on Dr. E's project, both international students.

"How long have you worked for Dr. E?" The Dean asks. He swills the water in his glass, sniffs as if it were fine wine.

"Since August of last year."

A cough ascends from his chest. He takes a sip from the glass.

"How much does he pay you?"

Dr. E made it a point to emphasize he pays me more than the minimum wage of three dollars and thirty-five cents.

"Five dollars an hour. I work evenings, twelve hours a week. In fact, he just paid me yesterday."

I dig into my backpack, feel for the crackle of notes, hand him the envelope.

Dean Wise holds the hundred-dollar bill up to the fluorescent light.

"Do you know some call these Franklins or Bens? Ha, ha!" The laugh irritates his respiratory passages, sets off a cough.

"You didn't think it was unusual, not receiving a check from the university, getting cash instead?" he asks.

I lick the cut on my lip. He hasn't mentioned The Payne.

He places the bills back into the envelope. "Young lady, I'm sorry, but yesterday was your last day of work."

Outside, the clickety-clack of Sara's typewriter stops.

"Dr. E is on administrative leave pending investigations."

"But I must graduate . . ."

The Dean's jowls shimmy, again. "You will. Go see Dr. Flambeau. That's all"

The cash sits on his desk. The money helps with groceries, with books, with utility payments.

I pick up the envelope.

I stop at Sara's desk. "Dr. E's gone?"

She waves me closer. "The research Dr. E conducted was personal, not sanctioned by the school. He used the school's resources, phone lines, the computer center . . ." Her phone rings. "Sorry," she mouths, as she picks up the receiver.

On my way out of the building, I read the new nameplate on Dr. E's office. I don't stop to introduce myself.

In my apartment, I knock on the wall between Theo's place and mine.

Another Letter from Amma

Calcutta
March 10, 1982

Dearest Deepa,

I meant to write this letter last night, but we had a power cut. You know how it is here. The situation is worse these days. We lose electricity frequently and randomly, which means I may be in the middle of grinding a chutney in the mixie when the power goes off. What's worse is that the building's water pump also stops, which means no water flows from the taps. If these outages were scheduled, I could plan better, make sure I store enough water to bathe and cook.

Thank God for Mr. Sen, the neighbor who lives across from us. As if he understands just what I need, he brings me batteries or a bucket of water. He says he's concerned because I'm alone, you see.

Yesterday, I went to the market to purchase some essentials. When I returned with my bags full of provisions (the usual mung dal, parboiled rice, chana, Parle biscuits, some brinjals, and curry leaves) the lift wasn't working. Of course, we had no power. I waited for fifteen minutes, pressing the button again and again, as if the lift would magically open. It didn't. So eventually, I took the stairs. After just one flight of stairs, I had to pause to catch my breath. Mr. Sen came, took my hand and my bags, and helped me home.

Which brings me to the point of this letter.

Mr. Sen says the Guptas who rent the apartment on the ground floor are moving. I tried to talk to the owners of the flat but the man asked me so many questions. What is my husband's name, where does he work, how much does he make per month? It's 1982 and this man doesn't want to rent to a widow because he doesn't believe she can pay.

Anyway, Mr. Sen says he will negotiate on my behalf. He wants to show them my bank statements. He also says if he mentions that my daughter lives in America, they will agree.

I told him I don't think I can walk up three flights of stairs anymore, so I'm willing to do anything to convince the owners.

The efficient Mr. Sen has already found a moving company. All they have to do is bring the furniture, the refrigerator, and the cupboards downstairs.

You should focus on your final project. I understand you have to explain your work? Will they ask you many questions? I am confident you will excel.

I hope to sign the lease by the time this letter reaches you. I wanted to tell you about the likely move so you can put the correct flat number, G-A instead of 3-A, on your letters from next month.

I like G-A. It sounds like an abbreviation for good abode.

Please write soon.

I hope you're eating well and sleeping well.

I know, I know, I say this at the end of every letter. I can hear your exasperated sigh.

Well, what can I say? I'm your mother and I worry about you.

Your loving, Amma

Bridge Across Oceans

You drive me to the airport after I clean my apartment and return the keys to the office. Blinding sunshine reflects off the chipped blue paint of your car. You roll the driver's side window half-way down; the stuttering air-conditioning doesn't work on this sweltry summer day.

On the way—breath hovering by the roof of my mouth—I wait for your words, my throat arid. I reach for your hand, so we can intertwine fingers as we did that afternoon when the President was shot. You extend an arm to turn on the radio instead, where someone's singing about a crazy little thing called love. Dissatisfied with the choices offered, you fiddle and fiddle with the knob changing five stations before you turn the device off.

Twelve minutes into the ride, I break the silence. The spate of words inside me wants to flood the car. I say you're the first person I met in this country and it's fitting that you should be taking me to the airport. I also say you can turn down your television—I won't be placing my ear against the wall between our apartments.

You don't respond.

A nervous giggle breaks loose. I apologize for forgetting my cardboard box of books in your apartment, the university texts for which I've paid hundreds of dollars. I request you to mail the package to India even as I cross my fingers hoping you'll repack the contents, read the note I've left you.

Your answer is not what I expect.

You say you'll move the window box over to your apartment so my quail, Dear-Moti-Chotu-Bobby-Sam, can continue to have his treats. When I thank you, you say the quail will miss me and isn't it strange that he's been visiting of late.

Minutes of awkward-quiet prickle.

I ask you to keep my typewriter, dig for a response. You tell me you'll sell the machine back to Gladys. I fake laugh and say she won't give you a penny. You say you wouldn't bet on it.

I know you like your bets and remind you about that time you bet your spicy omelet at our cafe would taste better than mine, when your eyes teared from the piercing heat of the jalapenos. I don't say it's the same place where we sat in a corner booth, shoulders flirting, elbows caressing.

You say an eyelash swam in your eye.

I watch you focus on the traffic ahead as if there's nothing more to say, as if you didn't bring me pumpkin pie, smile sparkling, as if you didn't hold me when my teary-tired body wanted to crumple on Thanksgiving

Day, as if you didn't become disappointed-angry when I didn't spend Christmas with you and your family.

You drum your fingers on the steering wheel.

I ask, again, why you can't comprehend I must go. My mind harbors disquiet about my mother, about sleazy Mr. Sen—it terrifies me when he answers her phone. You say Amma is a mature adult who knows what she's doing. I describe, again, how unworldly she is, how alone, how ill; how I have a responsibility. You open your fist, study the map of lines in your palm, say you don't know how to build a bridge across oceans.

You pull up to the curb at the airport.

A chill whips my skin when I realize you won't walk me to the gate. I crave a kiss to have, to hold, to cherish.

I reach for you after you get my bags out of the trunk. You put your arms around me, rest your chin on my head and say, "Bye, have a good life."

The words arc their way into my ears, then sink—like crumbling boulders—all the way into my toes. You slide your long legs into the driver's seat and adjust your glasses before you belt yourself in. Your arm sticks out of the open window as you wave goodbye.

Thirty thousand feet above earth, I adjust and readjust the airline's flimsy, child-sized blanket over cold arms, close my eyes.

I map your drive home, where you will unpack and repack my box, find my invitation to meet Amma—because it's time I told Amma about you, it's time I told Amma everything.

About the Author

Sudha Balagopal's fiction straddles continents and cultures, blending thoughts and ideas from the East and the West. She is the author of a novel, *A New Dawn*, and two short story collections, *There are Seven Notes* and *Missing and Other Stories*.

Her short fiction has been published in journals around the world, been nominated for the Pushcart Prize and Best Small Fictions, will appear in Best Microfiction 2021 and is listed in the Wigleaf Top 50. When she's not writing, she teaches yoga.

More at www.sudhabalagopal.com

Acknowledgments

Many thanks to the Bath Novella-in-Flash Award team. Without their competition, this novella would not have come to life. I am grateful to Ad Hoc Fiction for publishing this story—such a privilege to be a part of their world.

Thank you, thank you, judge Michelle Elvy, for selecting my novella as highly commended. I am truly honored.

I am indebted to Gillian Walker, Sara Siddiqui Chansarkar, Dan Crawley and Lavanya Vasudevan for their feedback and comments that helped hone this story.

I am also grateful to the members of the West Valley Writer's Critique Group for their unstinting support over the years.

Many thanks to Jim Painter for the wonderful cover design.

Finally, much love to my husband and my children for their support and encouragement.

My gratitude to the following journals for publishing individual chapters from this novella:

Things I Can't Tell Amma first appeared in Split Lip Magazine, Feb 14, 2020.

Quail With a Topknot first appeared in Smokelong Quarterly, September 28, 2020

The Missing "I" first appeared in Fictive Dream, October 2, 2020.

Printed in Great Britain
by Amazon